This Little Tiger book
belongs to:

_____

_____

_____

For Andy, who sometimes wakes up grumpy
(but mostly lets her sleep) – SS

For Phils . . . play on – CP

LITTLE TIGER PRESS
An imprint of Magi Publications
1 The Coda Centre
189 Munster Road, London SW6 6AW
www.littletigerpress.com

First published in Great Britain 2010
This edition published 2010
Text copyright © Steve Smallman 2010
Illustrations copyright © Caroline Pedler 2010
Steve Smallman and Caroline Pedler have asserted their rights
to be identified as the author and illustrator of this work
under the Copyright, Designs and Patents Act, 1988
A CIP catalogue record for this book
is available from the British Library
All rights reserved

ISBN 978-1-84895-033-7
Printed in Belgium • LTP/1300/0128/0910
10 9 8 7 6 5 4 3 2 1

Don't Wake the Bear, Hare!

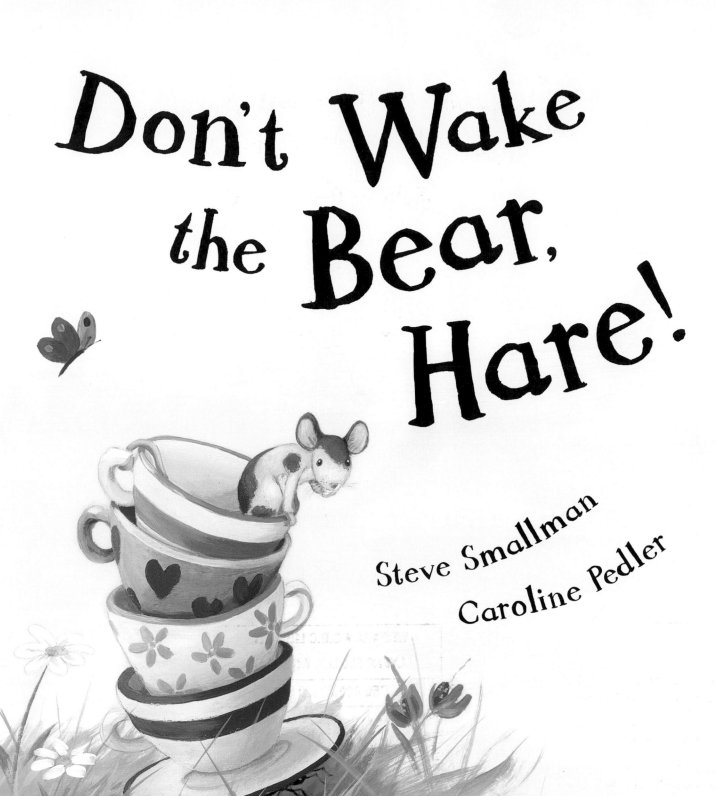

Steve Smallman

Caroline Pedler

LITTLE TIGER PRESS

London

It was Spring Party Day, the best day of the year,

So why were the animals trembling with fear?

They'd heard growly noises and crept up to see ...

A huge bear asleep in the old hollow tree!

"Oh no!" they all cried. "But our party's today!
How can we get ready with **him** in the way?"
"**I'll wake him up!**" cried a little brown hare.
"No, no!" they all whispered. "Please, don't wake the bear!"

zzzZZZ ZZZZZz

"Bears," Badger said, "are **enormous** and **hairy**.
If you wake them up they get angry and **scary!**
We'll **still** have our party, though, if we take care.
Be quiet as mice so we **don't** wake the bear!"

So they tippy-toed off without making a peep,
To fetch party things while the bear was asleep.
And the ants carried wibbling, wobbling stacks
Of dishes and saucers and cups on their backs.

The lanterns were **carefully** hung in the trees.
The mice **tied** up ribbons that danced on the **breeze**.
They brought in the very last **blueberry** tart
And **their party** was now almost ready to start!

Then Hare cried, "There's only **one** thing left to do!"
And he grabbed a **balloon** and he blew and he blew,

And he **blew** and he **blew** till the others cried, "STOP!
If it gets any **bigger** it's going to–"

The bear **stretched** and **groaned** and they all held their breath,
Then his eyes **flickered** open and scared them to death!
"**Run**, run and hide!" they all cried in despair.
"Now we're in trouble, we've **woken** the **bear!**"

"WHO DARES WAKE ME UP?"

growled the bear angrily.

Hare said in a small shaky voice,
"It was me!
Our party is going to start very soon,
I was trying to **help**, but I popped my balloon . . ."

"A party?" cried Bear, with a grin. "Could it be?
A big surprise party especially for me?

"Oh, **thank you** for waking me up, little bunny.
I'll come to your party and bring you some **honey!**"

And even though Bear was enormous and hairy,
They found he was great **fun** and not a bit scary.
He **danced** and he partied with everyone there,
And they all cheered, "Hurray for our new **friend**, the bear!"

Get ready to party with these books from Little Tiger Press!

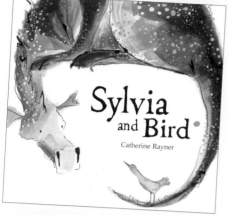

Sylvia and Bird
Catherine Rayner

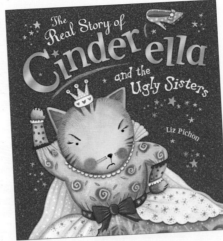

The Real Story of **Cinderella** and the **Ugly Sisters**
Liz Pichon

Rhino's Great BIG Itch!
Natalie Chivers

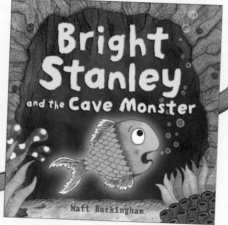

Bright Stanley and the **Cave Monster**
Matt Buckingham

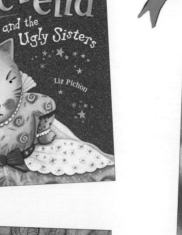

WHAT'S MORE SCARY THAN A SHARK?
Paul Bright   Michael Terry

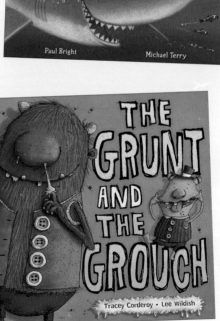

THE GRUNT AND THE GROUCH
Tracey Corderoy • Lee Wildish

For information regarding any of the above titles
or for our catalogue, please contact us:
Little Tiger Press, 1 The Coda Centre,
189 Munster Road, London SW6 6AW
Tel: 020 7385 6333 • Fax: 020 7385 7333
E-mail: info@littletiger.co.uk • www.littletigerpress.com